MEL BAY PRESENTS

Violin
Tune Book

POCKETBOOK DELUXE SERIES
by William Bay

1 2 3 4 5 6 7 8 9 0

Table of Contents

Haul Away, Joe

Green Grow the Lilacs

Tenting Tonight

Aloha Oe

Lament

The Foggy, Foggy Dew

The Ash Grove

One More River

Auld Lang Syne

12 **Strawberry Roan**

Johnny Has Gone
for a Soldier

Ol' Dan Tucker

Blow Away
the Morning Dew

Bell Bottom Trousers

Old Shoe Boots
& Leggins

Wait Till the
Sun Shines Nellie

At a Georgia
Camp Meeting

Marchin' to Glory

Goin' South

Oh, Sinner Man

24 Come & Go with Me
to that Land

Bile' Dem Cabbage Down

Goober Peas

Captain Kidd

The Fish of the Sea

Jolly Old Roger

My Bonnie

The Bold Fisherman

High Barbaree

Greenland Fishery

Blow, Ye Winds

Cripple Creek

Sourwood Mountain

Big Rock Candy Mountain

The Roving Cowboy

When Jesus Wept

Blessed Quietness

There's a River of Life

When I Can Read My Title Clear

Early American

Praise the Savior

Great God When I Approach Thy Throne

Early American

Must Jesus Bear
The Cross Alone

I am Bound for
the Promised Land

When Jesus Left
His Father's Throne

Jesus Calls Us

Lonesome Valley

The Galway Races

Cockles & Mussels

The Wild Rover

Love is Teasin'

The Galway Shawl

The Rose of Tralee

Brian O'linn

Spancil Hill

Si Beag Si Mór

Bunclody

My Mary of the Curling Hair

Musetta's Waltz

Drink to Me Only
with Thine Eyes

Southern Roses

Strauss

Gypsy Theme

Hatikvoh

Israeli

Santa Lucia

Tis So Sweet

Gospel Song

68 I Need Thee Every Hour

Gospel Song

Precious Memories

Gospel Song

Mandy Lee

American Ballad

Daisy Bell

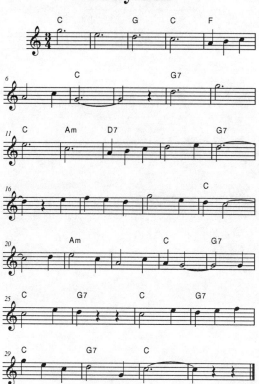

Up in a Balloon

Strike Up the Band

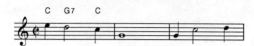

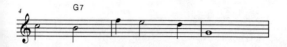

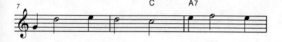

⁷⁴ This Little Light of Mine

Silver Threads
Among the Gold

Grandfather's Clock

All God's Children
Got Shoes

Little David Play
on Your Harp

If You're Happy
and You Know it

I've Got Peace Like a River

Spiritual

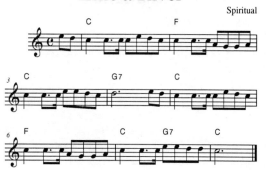

Bringing in the Sheaves

In the Pines

The Battle Cry
of Freedom

Nine Hundred Miles

Down Where the Cotton
Blossoms Grow

Lively Tempo   American Song

America the Beautiful

Our Boys will Shine Tonight

Columbia, the Gem
of the Ocean

Mama Don't 'Low

She'll Be Comin' Round
the Mountain

Loch Lomond

Crawdad Song

The Mermaid

American Sailing Song

The Old Oaken Bucket

Doxology